SPACE SCHOOL

CRASH COURSE

D1079074

For Mum, for putting up with us both.

First published 2011 by
A & C Black Publishers Ltd
36 Soho Square, London, W1D 3QY

www.acblack.com

Text copyright © 2011 Tony Bradman and Tom Bradman
Illustrations copyright © 2011 Si Clark

The rights of Tony Bradman, Tom Bradman and Si Clark to be
identified as the authors and illustrator of this work have been
asserted by them in accordance with the Copyrights,
Designs and Patents Act 1988.

ISBN 978-1-4081-2377-5

A CIP catalogue for this book is available from the British Library.

All rights reserved. No part of this publication may be
reproduced in any form or by any means – graphic, electronic
or mechanical, including photocopying, recording, taping or
information storage and retrieval systems – without
the prior permission in writing of the publishers.

This book is produced using paper that is made from wood
grown in managed, sustainable forests. It is natural, renewable and
recyclable. The logging and manufacturing processes conform
to the environmental regulations of the country of origin.

Printed and bound in Great Britain
by CPI Cox & Wyman, Reading, RG1 8EX.

SPACE SCHOOL

CRASH COURSE

Tom & Tony Bradman

Illustrated by Si Clark

A & C Black • London

LEWISHAM	
LIBRARY SERVICE	
	LOC:
PETERS	JF
16-Apr-2012	

CHAPTER ONE
UNDER ATTACK!

The first thing Luke saw when he came home from school was the message Mum had left on the wall-screen of their quarters. It was the usual stuff – she would be late yet again, please sort out the dinner, make sure you do your homework, boring, boring, blah, blah, blah.

Luke sighed. Life on the United Earth Spaceship *Buzz Aldrin* wasn't a bundle of laughs, especially when you were the captain's son. In fact, it was hard work, and recently he'd been so bored he could scream. Although, as Mum wasn't around now, at least his homework could wait...

Luke pulled the battered old games console out of his school bag and turned it on. While he waited for it to boot up, he got two space-meals ready. He put them in the auto-chef and jabbed at the timer buttons, not really looking at what he was doing as he thought about which game to play. It had to be *Ishtreen Attack*, he decided as he went into his tiny cabin and put on his headphones. It was the only game he still hadn't managed to finish. Soon he was sitting on his bunk, happily absorbed, time slipping by unnoticed.

Captain Luke pulled back on the joystick, dodging the explosions that blossomed around his small craft as he flew towards the Ishtreen mother-ship, a gigantic hulk of black metal, spiky with weapon tubes. The aliens had come to enslave the human race and only Captain Luke – the best

fighter pilot in the Solar System – could defeat them. He lined up the alien ship in his sights...

Suddenly, Luke's headphones were yanked off his ears. He hadn't heard Mum come in, and now she was standing there, giving him one of her 10-megaton glares.

This was not good. An angry mum was scarier than a thousand Ishtreen battle cruisers. A *lot* scarier. And what was that awful burning smell?

'So much for you sorting out dinner,' said Mum. She held up a plate with two blackened lumps in the middle of it. 'As far as I can tell, the auto-chef was on full power for an hour. I'm amazed it didn't burn a hole through the hull.'

'It's not my fault,' muttered Luke. 'Maybe it's broken or something.'

'Oh, just like it's not your fault that your grades at school have taken a dive, I suppose?' said Mum. She was tall and had short dark hair, very similar to Luke's. 'I bet you haven't even started your homework, have you?'

'Er... I was about to, honest...' Luke murmured, his voice trailing away.

'Really? I don't think so,' said Mum. 'You'd have played that stupid computer game all night if I hadn't come home. Can't you see they're a complete waste of time?'

'No, they're not!' said Luke. 'They're fun, and *I* don't see what's wrong with enjoying yourself. I think you can learn a lot from computer games, too.'

'Like what?' snapped Mum, crossing her arms and raising her eyebrows.

'Well... er...' Luke stammered, but he knew he was beaten.

'I see we're in agreement about *something* then,' said Mum, although her face had softened a little. She sighed. 'What am I going to do with you, Luke? You really need to start taking things a bit more seriously, you know...' And soon she had settled into Parent Lecture Mode, droning on and on.

Luke let his mind go blank. Giving him lectures was something his mum did a lot, and there was no point arguing with her. Not that she'd always been so grim and grumpy. They'd had loads of fun together back in the old days, when she'd just been a regular pilot on the Jupiter mining transports. But then all the bad stuff had happened on Earth...

Pollution had reached a critical level, the seas had risen and wiped out whole countries, and the air had become unbreathable. A few thousand survivors had managed to escape on a dozen spaceships, but the ships had lost contact with each other, so the *Buzz Aldrin* might now be humanity's last hope. Now they were alone in the depths of space with huge challenges to face. So Luke understood that being

captain of the ship was stressful for his mum. But that didn't make it any easier to live with her moods.

'Anyway, I think I've made my point,' she was saying. 'Right, hand it over.'

Luke reluctantly gave her the console. He had a feeling it would be a long time before he got it back.

'Thank you,' she said. 'And tomorrow I'll ask Clarke to give you more homework. You need to get those grades up again.'

His mum left the cabin, a whiff of smoke trailing behind her, the door hissing shut.

More homework! How could she? Talk about attack of the mother-ship. Luke was filled with gloom darker than the blackness of space. It looked like he was going to achieve a record level of boredom over the next few days.

CHAPTER TWO
A LITTLE DATA CUBE

At breakfast the next morning, Mum was still quite grumpy with him. So Luke was relieved when the door buzzer went and he heard the voice of his friend Yasmin over the intercom. He grabbed his school bag and hit the button to open the door.

'Bye, Mum!' he said and hurried off, dragging Yasmin with him, their footsteps echoing on the metal deck of the gangway.

'Bye, Luke!' Mum called out. 'Just make sure you work hard today.'

'Yeah, yeah, whatever...' Luke muttered under his breath, scowling.

'Oh dear,' laughed Yasmin. She had

coffee-coloured skin and long straight brown hair that she was constantly brushing. 'Having a spot of parent trouble, are we?'

'It's no joke, Yasmin,' said Luke. 'Mum confiscated my games console and she's going to ask Clarke to give me more homework. Can you believe it? That's child cruelty! I should complain to someone about her.'

'You could talk to the captain,' said Yasmin with a mock-serious frown. 'Oh, whoops, I forgot... your mum *is* the captain.'

'Very funny,' said Luke. 'And there's me thinking you were my friend.'

The gangway led to a corridor busy with people. Luke and Yasmin turned into it and walked past a view-port looking out on the central axle of the Buzz Aldrin, bright stars twinkling beyond. At one end of the axle –

a kilometre-long gantry like an enormous crane – was the giant engine pod, its massive exhausts belching fire.

At the other end was the ship's guidance module, a huge structure resembling a colossal golf ball that contained the control deck, otherwise known as the bridge. Luke and Yasmin were on the great wheel that was kept spinning to create artificial gravity for the dozens of families living on the spaceship.

They arrived at school and Yasmin tapped in the entry code. The door hissed open, and they were greeted by a hologram of an elderly man with white hair and a droopy moustache. This was Clarke, Primary 1's computer-generated teacher. He was networked into the *Buzz Aldrin*'s main computer, and could take on the appearance of anyone in the ship's knowledge banks. Today he had apparently decided to look like Earth's most famous scientist, Albert Einstein.

The curved walls of the classroom were covered in screens showing pictures of galaxies and star systems, and scenes from Earth. Twenty or so children were sitting round tables, working away at computer terminals. There was a class for infants next door, and one for the older kids on the other side of the corridor.

'Good morning, Luke and Yasmin,' said Clarke. His voice was soft and friendly. 'Please take your seats. We're starting with a surprise science test.'

'Terrific,' murmured Luke, his shoulders slumping. 'That's all I need!'

They sat down at a table next to their friend Yuri, a skinny boy with red hair that stuck up as if he'd just suffered an electric shock. He had been hunched over his own terminal, concentrating on the screen, but now he looked round at his friends. He smiled, then frowned when he saw how glum Luke looked.

'What's wrong with him?' Yuri asked Yasmin.

'Mum trouble,' said Yasmin. 'She's taken away his games console.'

'Whoa, that *is* bad,' whispered Yuri. He was a total geek who loved games, too. 'But, hey, this might cheer you up.' He slipped Luke a little data cube. 'Plug it into your terminal and you'll be able to play any game you want. I've even built some  software into it that will keep what you're doing hidden from Clarke.'

'Cool, thanks, Yuri,' said Luke, plugging in the data cube.

It was Luke's best time at school for ages. While his classmates struggled with the science test, he fought the Ishtreen – although they were almost impossible to defeat. He had to use every gaming trick

he knew. At one point, he was forced to escape from an Ishtreen tractor beam by going for a slingshot move – flying incredibly fast and low round a moon, using its gravity to give his engine an extra boost of speed.

Finally, he realised there was only one way to complete the game. It would have to be a suicide mission.

Captain Luke aimed his fighter at the Ishtreen mother-ship on a crash course, then locked the navigation system with his secret password, 1CoolBoy. There was no backing out now. Soon those evil aliens would be destroyed in the biggest explosion the Solar System had ever seen. And he would be a hero!

Suddenly Luke heard a familiar voice, looked up from his terminal – and gulped. His mum had just walked into the classroom and was talking to Clarke.

CHAPTER THREE
SLIGHTLY FUZZY

Luke almost froze with panic. If Mum caught him playing a computer game when he was supposed to be doing a school test, his life wouldn't be worth living, not after what she'd said last night. He didn't have time to quit the game properly now. There was only one thing for it – he simply pulled out the data cube, palmed it to Yuri, and hit the re-boot button on his terminal.

The screen went blank then instantly shimmered into life again, although the log-on page didn't come up. Instead, an image of the Ishtreen mother-ship re-appeared with a stream of numbers running over it,

and at the same time all the lights in the classroom flickered. Luke saw his mum glance at them and frown, the way she did whenever she thought something was wrong on the *Buzz Aldrin*.

'That shouldn't happen,' Luke heard her say. 'I'd better get the maintenance crew to check out the ship's power cables... Hey, are you all right, Clarke?'

'Yes, I think so,' said Clarke. He had gone slightly pixelated, a little like a TV screen being scrambled by interference. 'Just a touch of indigestion, I think. At least, a quick scan of the ship's knowledge banks tells me that's what it's like.'

'How strange,' said Mum, looking concerned. 'I wasn't aware holograms suffered from that kind of thing. Perhaps I ought to get you checked out, too. Anyway, carry on, everyone. I mustn't stop you all from working.'

She turned to leave, but then she glanced at Luke and paused, biting her lip. Luke looked down and concentrated fiercely on his terminal, hoping she would hurry up and go. Even the tiniest glimpse of his screen would tell her what he had been doing... *But, oh no, she was coming towards him*!

Luke jabbed the re-boot button again and again, and at last the log-on page crackled into view. He got to the test just as Mum's hand landed on his shoulder.

'I'm pleased to see you working so hard, Luke,' she whispered, giving him one of

those encouraging I-Knew-You-Could-Do-It Smiles she specialised in. 'What's this, a science test? Wow, it certainly looks pretty challenging.'

'Piece of cake, Mum,' Luke whispered back. 'Just watch my grades go up.' He noticed several other kids were asking Clarke about their terminals or jabbing at the re-boot button as he had done, and felt his cheeks burning.

'That's my boy,' she laughed, and for a moment Luke thought his mum was going to say something else, but she seemed to change her mind. 'I'll leave you to it,' she said, squeezing his shoulder. 'Let's talk later.' Then she was gone.

'Are you OK, Luke?' said Yasmin.

Yuri was looking at him, too.

'Yeah, fine, thanks,' said Luke, although he was definitely feeling a bit rattled. It had

been a close thing, and the stuff with the lights and Clarke had been rather odd, to say the least. Mum had been behaving strangely, too. What was all that about *talking later*? She was probably planning yet another lecture... Then Luke grinned. He had got away with it!

'Ten minutes left, everyone,' said Clarke. He wasn't fuzzy any more, but he had a pained expression on his face and kept rubbing his holographic tummy.

Luke finished the last question just in time. He liked science, and he actually thought the test had been quite easy. They had a history lesson next, and Clarke morphed into a series of famous people from the past, which made the class laugh. Then morning school was over and the three friends went for lunch.

'I hope we get something tasty today,'

muttered Yasmin as they went into the dining area and joined the queue with the other kids. The food came from automated dispensers, and there were several Tidy-Bots – shiny dustbins on wheels with arms – to collect empty dishes and wipe down the tables.

'Don't hold your breath,' said Yuri, picking up a tray from the pile at the end of the counter. 'It'll probably be the usual space-muck. I'd give anything for a pizza. Or maybe a hamburger and fries. No, wait, strawberry ice cream...'

'Stop it!' said Yasmin. 'We haven't had a good meal since we left Earth!'

Luke felt the same as his friends, but he'd stopped listening to them. The food dispenser wasn't working properly. He was pretty sure he'd pushed the right buttons for his choice – high-protein space porridge with extra sweetener – but the machine was making peculiar noises. It whirred and clanked and sounded like someone gargling honey. Luke felt nervous and stepped away from it.

Which was just as well. For suddenly it started to fire out balls of mashed potato

in a steady stream, reminding Luke of a dangerous shower of meteorites the *Buzz Aldrin* had managed to avoid a while back.

But there was no avoiding the mash, not for some people, anyway.

CHAPTER FOUR
A BRIEF OVERLOAD

Within seconds, several kids in the queue were covered in mashed potato and the rest had dived under tables or behind chairs. The Tidy-Bots scurried around, bleeping furiously as they tried to do their job of cleaning up the mess, but they were soon overwhelmed by the unending stream of edible meteorites.

'Wow, I've never seen anything like this,' murmured Luke. He and his friends were sheltering behind the drinks dispenser. 'What's going on?'

'No idea,' said Yuri, shrugging. 'We could probably put a stop to it, though. Somebody just needs to turn the machine off.'

'Why would anyone want to do that?' said Luke, laughing. 'This is great! I haven't seen anything so funny in a long time.'

'Well *I'm* not enjoying it,' muttered Yasmin. 'Ugh, I have mashed potato in my hair *and on my favourite top*... Right, that's it, I'm going in!'

'Don't!' Luke and Yuri yelled together, but it was too late.

Yasmin grabbed a dinner tray and, using it as a shield to deflect the stream of mash, she moved towards the machine. Finally, she did a forward roll, then rose up and lashed out with a perfect Kung-Fu kick, hitting the power button with her foot. The mash instantly stopped coming, the machine powering down with a dying whine and what sounded like an electronic belch.

'Hey, that was pretty cool,' said Luke. 'And I feel so much safer now I know we

can rely on you to protect us from The Great Mashed-Potato Monster.'

Luke and Yuri laughed and high-fived each other, and Yasmin scowled. 'Don't count on it,' she growled. But she was soon laughing with them.

The maintenance crew arrived with more Tidy-Bots, and the clean-up began. All the dispensers were turned off, and the kids were given energy bars and juice-packs before being sent back to class. But Clarke was still unwell.

'I'm sorry, everyone, afternoon school is cancelled,' he said. 'I've got to go for an IT check. I *have* sorted out plenty of homework for you, though. And, as requested by Captain Riley, there's a little extra for you, Luke.'

'Unlucky, Luke,' said Yuri as they set off homewards down the wheel.

Luke heard a commotion behind them, and looked over his shoulder to see the maintenance crew hurrying into the older kids' classroom. Smoke was coming out of the door, but that wasn't unusual. The older kids often played all sorts of tricks and practical jokes on Aldiss, their own hologram teacher.

'Yeah, it's not fair – you should refuse to do it,' said Yasmin. 'Listen, why don't you two come to my place? We could hang out, watch a movie, chill...'

'Thanks, Yasmin, but I'd better go home,' said Luke. 'If Mum hears I've actually been having some fun, she'll probably explode. See you!'

Yuri and Yasmin said goodbye, too, and Luke trudged off home.

Back at their quarters, Luke noticed his mum had already set the timer on the

auto-chef, so he headed straight for his cabin and settled down to do his homework. There seemed to be an awful lot of it.

Mum returned even later than usual. She sat down in their tiny living room, and Luke could see she was tired. She looked rather worried as well.

'Phew, what a day!' she said. 'We've had problems all over the ship, stuff we've never experienced before. The maintenance crew

has been run off its feet. Still, they seem to be on top of things at the moment...' She paused and smiled at him. 'Anyway, that's enough of my troubles,' she said brightly, obviously making an effort to be more cheerful. 'Tell me about your day! Actually, seeing you at school this morning made me wonder if I've –'

'Er... what kind of problems, exactly?' Luke asked with a sense of unease.

'Oh, lots of strange things,' said Mum, frowning. 'Machines going crazy, terminals burning out, loads of computer glitches. We haven't managed to track down the cause yet, but we do know the trouble started this morning, at about the time I came to your class, oddly enough. We're beginning to think there might have been a brief overload in the ship's main computer around then.'

'An overload?' Luke squeaked, his skin going cold all over.

'That's right,' Mum said. She opened her mouth to say something else, but just then the incoming call buzzer sounded. Mum turned to the wall-screen.

'Could you come to the bridge, Captain Riley?' said First Officer Chung. She had short black hair and brown eyes, and was usually very calm. But now there was a look of mild panic on her face. 'We're having more problems.'

'I'm on my way,' said Mum. 'Sorry, Luke,' she sighed. 'Duty calls, I'm afraid.'

The door hissed shut behind her, and Luke stood there, frozen to the spot.

He had a bad feeling about all this, a very bad feeling indeed...

CHAPTER FIVE
OUT OF ORDER

Luke was fast asleep when Mum got back, so he didn't see her until breakfast the next morning. They didn't talk much – the captain was too busy taking a stream of calls from Chung about things going wrong all over the ship. Poor Clarke was still feeling unwell, and for a moment Luke thought he might get the day off school. But Mum had already found a new teacher for his class.

'I was going to ask the other hologram teachers to look after Primary 1 today, but they've had a few problems themselves,' said Mum as she scanned a report Chung had sent her. 'So Chief Engineer Asimov has volunteered to fill in. Engineering seems OK at the moment. Let's just hope it stays that way...'

Luke was deep in thought on the way to school with Yasmin, and hardly heard any of her cheery chatter. At lunchtime he and his friends went to the dining area, where all the food dispensers had signs on them saying OUT OF ORDER, and a Tidy-Bot was going round in circles, bleeping sadly. The friends collected their energy-bars and juice-packs and sat in their usual corner.

'OK, Luke, what's up?' said Yasmin. 'You've been looking as miserable as my little sister did when her hamster died. Is it your mum?'

'Er... not exactly,' Luke said quietly. 'Although if I'm right in what I'm thinking, she's going to go completely nuts.'

'Come on, then, out with it,' said Yuri. 'What in space are you on about?'

'You know the problems we've been having on the ship?' said Luke. His friends nodded. 'Mum told me they started around the time she came to our classroom. I'm wondering if they have anything to do with me turning off that data cube.'

'I don't see why,' said Yuri. Then he frowned. 'You *did* shut it down before pulling it out, didn't you? Please tell me you didn't leave it on...'

'Obviously he did,' said Yasmin. 'You can tell just by looking at his face!'

'It wasn't my fault,' muttered Luke, and Yasmin pulled a face at him. 'OK, I panicked,' he said. 'Just tell me how much damage it's done.'

'We won't know until I've hacked into the ship's main computer,' said Yuri. 'I'll need

you two to keep old Asimov distracted while I work my magic!'

It turned out that Chief Engineer Asimov could be distracted quite easily, mostly with questions about his years of service in the Space Corps. 'I'm *so* glad you asked me that,' he replied every time. 'I remember when I was on a deep-space run once...'

Yasmin turned to Luke and rolled her eyes, and Luke smiled. Mr Asimov paced the room while he talked, his long, skinny legs carrying him quickly from one side to the other. His thin grey hair got messier and messier as he scratched his head, trying to remember the technical details.

Meanwhile, Yuri worked away at his terminal. At the end of school, the three friends left together. But instead of going straight home, they headed for the hydroponics bay, the place where most of the ship's food was grown in great towers and racks, or under plastic domes. It was a good place to talk without being seen or overheard – there had been no glitches in any of its systems, so the bay would be empty except for the robots watering the crops.

'Bad news, I'm afraid,' Yuri said quietly, his face grim. 'Pulling out the data cube like that has de-stabilised the ship's AI core-routines.'

'Warning, geek-speak alert!' said Yasmin. 'Translation please, Yuri.'

Yuri sighed. 'Everything in the cube was instantly dumped into the ship's main computer, a bit like a virus,' he said slowly, as if he were speaking to a pair of complete idiots. 'That's why the lights flickered and Clarke felt ill.'

'And it's been spreading through the ship,' said Luke, starting to feel sick himself.

'Spot on, Luke,' said Yuri. But then he smiled. 'There is some good news, though. It should be easy for the tech guys to fix once they trace the source.'

'My terminal,' said Luke, his stomach churning. 'How long's that going to take?'

'It could be a day,' said Yuri. 'Or just a couple of hours.'

'Oh dear, Luke,' said Yasmin. 'Maybe it's time for you to own up.'

Luke thought about it. He tried to picture himself confessing. He tried to imagine his mum forgiving him. But neither of those things seemed possible. All he could see was a future in which the Tidy-Bots wouldn't have much to do. Mum would probably make him clean the ship from the engine to the bridge.

'Er... somehow I don't think that's an option,' he said. Then an idea struck him, and he smiled. 'Listen, if it's so easy to sort out – why can't *we* do it?'

CHAPTER SIX
SEARCH & DESTROY

'I'll need to go home for my laptop,' said Yuri, rubbing his chin. 'Then we'll have to find a terminal in a quiet part of the ship that will give us access to the main-frame – and that we have no links with. Luckily, I know just the place.'

'Great, let's get going!' said Luke. 'The sooner we sort this out, the better.'

Half an hour later, Yuri led his friends down a little-used service corridor to the ship's storage section. They stopped at last by some double doors and Yuri tapped in an entry code. The doors hissed open, and the children slipped into a large space filled with plastic crates stacked almost to the curved ceiling.

'What's in all these boxes?' murmured Yasmin, her eyes wide, her voice echoing off the metal walls and deck. Luke was surprised by them, too.

'Oh, just a lot of old stuff we saved from Earth, I think,' said Yuri. They had called in at his family's quarters on the way to collect his laptop, and now he was plugging it into a terminal on the wall beside the door. 'Statues, paintings... nothing useful. OK, the main-frame is asking for a password...'

Luke stood beside his friend, watching his fingers fly over the keyboard, numbers scrolling across the laptop's screen in seemingly endless lines.

'Er... what exactly are you going to do once you're in, Yuri?' he asked.

Yuri gave Luke a withering look. 'Upload my best search-and-destroy anti-virus programme, of course!' he snapped. 'What else did you think?'

'I was only asking,' muttered Luke. 'Are you sure it will do the job?'

'Hard to tell,' said Yuri, tapping away. 'We'll just have to wait and see.'

Yasmin snorted. 'Great!' she said. 'And we thought you were a genius.'

That evening, as he waited for his mum to get home, Luke felt like crossing all his fingers and toes – he was desperate for Yuri's anti-virus programme to work. He felt a twinge of guilt, too, knowing Mum had been put under even more stress than usual because of him. So, to make up for it, he decided to tidy his cabin. He also made sure that dinner would be ready – and not burned to a crisp – when she came in.

'This is nice!' said Mum as the door hissed shut behind her. Luke had set the table and put a vase of plastic flowers on it. 'What have you done now?'

'Er... n-nothing,' Luke spluttered, his cheeks turning red. 'Honest, I...'

'Don't worry, I was only joking,' said Mum, laughing. 'Come on, let's eat. I'm starving. This is the second day in a row I've missed out on lunch.'

Hearing that, Luke felt another twinge of guilt. But his mum was very relaxed, almost like her old self. Although after a while Luke began to sense she had something to say. He waited, his heart sinking, wondering what was coming.

'Listen, Luke,' she said quietly at last. 'I think I owe you an apology.'

'Really?' said Luke, taken aback. He hadn't expected that. 'What for?'

'Being grumpy,' she said. 'When I saw you working hard at school yesterday, I realised I've probably been a bit too tough on you lately. Life isn't easy for either of

us right now, but I shouldn't take out my moods on you...'

Mum kept talking, and Luke stared at her with a stiff grin on his face, his guilt stronger than ever. Mum was admitting she had been wrong, so shouldn't *he* come clean now in return, confess what he had done, apologise to *her*?

'Not to worry, Mum, I know you've been under a lot of pressure,' he said, steeling himself to tell her about the data cube. He took a deep breath. 'I –'

'You can say that again!' laughed Mum. 'Yesterday was a *nightmare*. But those glitches have stopped, thank goodness. The main computer somehow just sorted itself out. Everything is fine now, even Clarke is feeling a lot better.'

'That's great,' said Luke. He wanted to leap to his feet and punch the air, and his desire to confess vanished like a meteor plunging into a black hole.

'Anyway, I think we both deserve a treat after the last few days,' said Mum. 'So you can forget about doing homework this evening – let's chill out and watch a movie together instead, like we used to. I'm not giving you that games thingy back yet, though. Not until I see your school grades getting up to where they were before.'

Luke was about to say he would definitely try his best at school from now on – but suddenly the whole of their quarters seemed to tip over at a steep angle. The vase fell off the table and smashed on the metal deck, and an ear-splitting alarm started going *WHOOP-WHOOP* in the gangway outside.

'*EMERGENCY!*' intoned the voice of the ship's computer. '*RED ALERT...*'

Luke and his mum had been sent flying across the cabin and ended up in a heap against the wall. Their plates had fallen off the table and smashed, too. In fact, everything that wasn't bolted down had come loose. But gradually the deck began to level out, allowing them to untangle themselves and get to their feet.

'Are you OK, Luke?' Mum asked, her face full of concern.

'Er … yeah, I think so,' said Luke.

His mum smiled and gave him a hug. Then she put on her serious I'm-The-Captain face, and turned to the wall-screen.

'Captain Riley calling the bridge,' she said. 'What the heck is going on?'

'We're not sure, Captain,' replied Chung, her eyes wide. There was a large stain down the front of her uniform, and Luke realised she must have been holding a cup of coffee when the *Buzz Aldrin* had tipped over. 'All we know is that the ship's computer is behaving rather strangely, to say the least!'

Luke felt a surge of anxiety. He crossed his fingers once more, hoping this had nothing to do with the data cube. But he had a nasty feeling that it did.

'What are you talking about, Chung?' Mum said, frowning. 'Just then it felt as if we suddenly changed course. And why are we putting on so much speed?'

Everyone on board the ship could tell how fast the *Buzz Aldrin* was going by the throbbing in the deck beneath their feet. Now Luke noticed it was more intense than it had ever been, and was growing stronger by the second.

'No idea, Captain,' said Chung. 'The computer seems to be in a hurry to get us somewhere. Oh, and it's locked us out of the navigation system as well, so at the moment we can't change course back again, although we *are* trying.'

'OK, I'm on my way,' Mum said, her frown deepening. 'Sorry, Luke, but I have to go. Can I leave you to clean up in here and look after yourself?'

'No problem, Mum,' said Luke.

The second the door hissed shut behind his mum, Luke called Yuri and Yasmin on the video-screen. He arranged to meet them at the storage hold, then hurried off through a ship in total chaos. Every corridor and gangway was littered with things that had fallen down or sprung loose when the *Buzz Aldrin* had suddenly changed course.

Yasmin and Yuri were already at the hold when Luke arrived. Yuri had his laptop plugged into the same terminal as before, and was scowling.

'What's happened?' said Luke. 'Didn't your anti-virus programme work?'

'Of course it did,' said Yuri, the screen

lighting up his face. 'That's the problem. It cleaned up the secondary systems, which is why the minor glitches stopped. But in doing so it pushed the virus even deeper into the main-frame.'

'More geek-speak,' muttered Yasmin. 'No one understands you, Yuri.'

'The ship's main computer has been taken over by the game Luke was playing when he pulled out the data cube,' said Yuri. He tapped away at the keyboard and nodded at what came onto the laptop's screen. 'There you go – it thinks it's in the final level of the game, attacking some alien spacecraft.'

'The Ishtreen mother-ship,' groaned Luke. It was there in all its glory on the screen, a familiar gigantic hulk of black metal, spiky with weapon tubes. 'But hang on a minute – that's what the computer

thinks it's seeing, right? It's not real, is it? So how come the computer made the ship change course?'

'The ship's scanners must have picked up something nearby that looks like the Ishtreen mother-ship,' said Yuri. 'Hold on, I'll see if I can bypass the computer itself and pull up what the scanners are actually showing.'

Yuri's fingers flew over the keyboard. The laptop's screen shimmered and a new image appeared – one which looked a lot like the Ishtreen mother-ship.

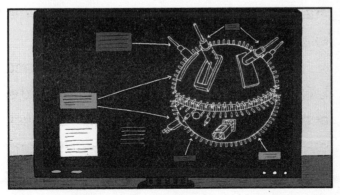

'What is *that*?' said Luke, peering at the screen. 'Some kind of planet?'

'More like a rogue moon,' said Yuri. 'Solid metal, and probably radioactive. And I hate to say this, but the *Buzz Aldrin* seems to be minutes from crashing into it.'

'Oh no...' Luke moaned. 'I realised the only way to finish the game was to crash into the mother-ship. I set the course just before I pulled out the cube.'

'Something tells me we're in big trouble,' said Yasmin. 'There's going to be quite a bang when we hit that piece of rock. What are they doing on the bridge?'

'Chung is trying to regain control of navigation,' said Yuri. 'But she's getting nowhere. I assume you locked it with your password in the game, Luke.'

'What if I give *you* the password?' said Luke. 'Can you unlock it from here?'

'That would take too long,' said Yuri. 'It would be better if you put your password directly into the terminal on the bridge.'

Luke didn't need telling twice. He dashed out of the room.

CHAPTER EIGHT
TERRIBLE DANGER

Luke ran through the *Buzz Aldrin* as fast as he could go. He headed for the bridge, yelling 'GANGWAY!' at the top of his voice, his space boots clanging on the decks. But his mind was moving even faster than his feet. Things looked bad. Everyone on the ship might die because of him – the people in the corridors, the kids in his school, Asimov, Chung, even Mum... He had to get to the bridge in time – and he had to tell Mum the truth, whatever the consequences.

On the bridge he was greeted by the familiar sight of Mum in her captain's seat, and Asimov and Chung standing at their terminals, which were endless panels of switches and lights. The image on the huge forward view-screen was familiar, too – although it was strange to see it on such a large scale. The Ishtreen mother-ship almost filled the whole screen, and it was growing larger with every passing nano-second.

'*THREE MINUTES TO IMPACT...*' intoned the voice of the computer.

'I just don't get it,' Chung was saying, her voice full of frustration. 'A huge alien spaceship appears out of nowhere, blazing away and not hitting us. But then our computer decides to attack and heads for it on a crash course...'

'Er, actually, I can explain,' said Luke, and all eyes on the bridge turned to him.

At that moment Yasmin came running in, a breathless Yuri behind her.

'What are you doing here, Luke?' said a puzzled Mum. 'And what do you mean you can explain? We've got a serious problem here, this is no time to –'

'You'd better listen to him, Captain,' panted Yuri. 'Or we're all toast.'

'OK, Luke, talk,' said Mum, scowling now. 'You've got ten seconds.'

Luke took a deep breath, then told her everything as quickly as he could, gabbling the words – playing a computer game in class... pulling out the little data cube without quitting... Yuri uploading an anti-virus programme into the ship's computer... the terrible danger they were in. 'I know I shouldn't have done any of it, and I'm really sorry,' he said at last.

Mum stared at him, and for a brief instant it was as if they were the only two people on the bridge. 'I suppose I should be cross with you,' she said quietly. 'And don't think you're going to get away with it completely. I'll be having a word with your friends' parents, too,' she added, giving Yuri and Yasmin a stern look. Then she sighed. 'But you might have just saved the *Buzz Aldrin*... so if you give me your password, we'll call it quits. For now.'

'Whatever you say, Mum,' said Luke.

Soon Chung was punching *1CoolBoy* into the computer's terminal. Lights flickered into life on more panels and two joysticks rose out of the arms of Mum's seat, one for each hand. She gripped hold of them, and Luke could feel a subtle change in the ship – Mum was back in control.

'*TWO MINUTES TO IMPACT...*' intoned the voice of the computer.

'I'm going to need all the power you can give me, Mr Asimov,' she said.

'I'm afraid we've been at maximum power for a while, Captain, and that won't do the engines any good at all,' said Asimov. 'I remember once on a –'

'Any change in our course yet, Chung?' said Mum. Luke could feel the deck juddering beneath his fee – the *Buzz Aldrin* was under colossal strain.

'No, Captain,' said Chung. 'Something seems to be pulling us down.'

'It's a rogue moon,' said Yuri. 'The scanners think it's the ship in the game, but that doesn't matter. We're probably caught in its gravitational field now.'

'*SIXTY SECONDS TO IMPACT...*' intoned the voice of the computer.

Chung did something to her terminal, and suddenly the forward view-screen shimmered. The Ishtreen mother-ship vanished and was instantly replaced by an image of what was really out there in space. The rogue moon filled the whole screen, its surface pitted with rocky craters, giving off a faintly evil glow.

Everyone on the bridge gasped at the sight – everyone except Mum. Luke could see her concentrating, fighting hard to save the ship and its precious cargo of

humanity. Then suddenly he thought about what Yuri had just said.

'There's a way *you* can save us, Mum!' he said. 'You have to go for the old slingshot move, using the moon's gravity to give us an extra boost of speed.'

'I know what a slingshot move is, Luke,' said Mum, turning to look at him in surprise. 'But how in space do you? Plenty of pilots haven't even heard of it.'

'It's something I came across a while back... in a stupid computer game,' said Luke with a straight face. 'You'd be amazed at what you can learn from them.'

'Is that so?' said Mum, raising an eyebrow. 'I had no idea they were so educational.'

'Er... I don't want to interrupt,' said Yasmin. 'But could you like, hurry up and save us?'

'Don't worry, I'm just about to,' said Mum. 'Hold tight, everyone.'

'*TEN SECONDS TO IMPACT...*' intoned the voice of the computer. '*NINE, EIGHT...*' Luke grabbed the arm of Mum's seat as she fired the thrusters, getting the *Buzz Aldrin* lined up for its final approach. The ship screamed down towards the moon and skimmed just above the surface like a tiny fly circling a football. It went nearly all the way around... then the moon's gravity kicked in and sent the ship whizzing safely off into space at over a thousand kilometres a second.

'*IMPACT AVOIDED WITH ONE SECOND TO GO,*' intoned the voice of the computer.

Cheers broke out on the bridge, and Mum gave Luke's hand a squeeze. 'Maybe you should show me this game of yours,' she said, smiling at him. 'Could the two of us play on your console thingy together?'

'Sure,' said Luke with a huge grin.

Maybe life on the *Buzz Aldrin* wasn't so bad after all.